Spells
and Smells

Collect all the Naughty Fairies books:

Spells
and Smells

Lucy Mayflower

Hodder
Children's
Books

A division of Hachette Children's Books

Special thanks to Lucy Courtenay

Created by Hodder Children's Books and Lucy Courtenay
Text and illustrations copyright © 2006 Hodder Children's Books
Illustrations created by Artful Doodlers

First published in Great Britain in 2006
by Hodder Children's Books

3

A Catalogue record for this book is available from the British Library

ISBN – 10: 0 340 91182 4
ISBN – 13: 978 0 340 91182 2

Printed and bound in Great Britain
by Bookmarque Ltd, Croydon, Surrey

The paper and board used in this paperback by Hodder Children's Books
are natural recyclable products made from wood grown in
sustainable forests. The manufacturing processes conform to the
environmental regulations of the country of origin.

Hodder Children's Books
A division of Hachette Children's Books
338 Euston Rd, London NW1 3BH

Contents

Ambrosia Academy

WOOD STUMP

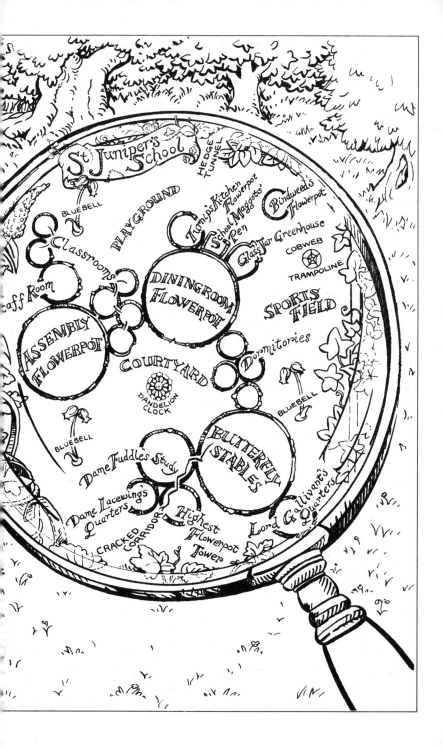

1

Pixie Post

Down at the bottom of the garden, the autumn wind was blowing hard. It whistled around the flowerpot towers of St Juniper's school for fairies, wriggling through the windows and the cracks in the walls.

In the Dining Flowerpot, the fairies were having breakfast. Leaf plates jumped off the tables and clover buns flew around the room like small missiles. Any fairies who had forgotten to furl their wings properly were blown off their benches. It was dangerous weather.

Dame Fuddle, Head of St Juniper's, stood up at the staff table and waved her wand. Sparks jumped and cracked through the air. "Good morning, my fairies!" Dame Fuddle raised her voice to make herself heard over the wind. "I have several notices this morning! Firstly, Lord Gallivant has cancelled today's flying lessons!"

Dame Fuddle often spoke in exclamation marks.

"Typical," snorted a pretty fairy with skin the colour of chocolate, who was sitting with her five friends at a table nearest the door. "Windy weather's the best for flying. Remember what happened to Lord Gallivant last time?"

"He couldn't even get off the ground, could he, Brilliance?" said the smallest fairy cheerfully.

"That was the time before last, Tiptoe," corrected a blonde, short-haired fairy with a smudge of dirt on her chin. "Last time, he ended up in the ivy fence."

2

"Did he?" asked a spiky-haired fairy with interest. "What happened, Nettle?"

"Oh, you weren't at St Juniper's then, were you, Ping?" said Nettle. She twiddled her tiny spider earrings. "The wind stuck him to the fence like glue. He stayed up there for most of the lesson. It was great."

"Lord Gallivant said he did it on purpose, to show us the dangers of windy days," said a round-faced fairy

who was sitting at the far end of the table. There was a shiny little ladybird asleep on her lap.

"Yeah, right," snorted a red-haired fairy in a long black and yellow dress. "You didn't believe him, did you, Sesame?"

"Of course I didn't, Kelpie," said Sesame, after a short pause. "It's just what he *said*, that's all."

There was a hungry buzzing sound from somewhere near Kelpie's feet.

"Sounds like Flea's awake," said Nettle.

Kelpie passed a bit of honeycake under the table. The buzzing stopped.

"What's Flea doing down there?" Brilliance asked.

"Keeping my feet warm," said Kelpie. "Furry bumblebees are useful like that."

Up at the staff table, Dame Fuddle was still talking.

". . . this afternoon I will be

representing St Juniper's at SPARCLE – the Senior Peris' Annual Reunion Conference for Learning and Education! It is a great honour to be invited, and I'm sure that I take the good will of St Juniper's with me!"

"What's a peri?" Tiptoe whispered.

"A posh fairy," Kelpie said, passing another piece of honeycake under the table to Flea.

". . . and lastly," said Dame Fuddle, "I'm delighted to announce that my sister, Dame Cavity, is taking a break from her busy life as Regional Tooth Fairy! She is coming to visit us at St Juniper's today before a vital tooth mission up at the House!"

A burst of chatter followed this announcement. Dame Cavity was a Very Important Fairy.

"Dame Cavity will be just in time for Dame Fuddle's flutterday tomorrow," said Kelpie.

Flutterdays were the fairy equivalent of birthdays.

"Dame Fuddle's sister always comes for Dame Fuddle's flutterday," Nettle told Ping. "She had ten clover buns, five pieces of rose-hip toast and three helpings of scrambled ants' eggs for the flutterday breakfast last year. We counted."

"Don't forget the sugared buttercups," Brilliance added.

"Or the mint twists," Sesame agreed.

"If fairies ever lost their teeth, Dame Cavity would have lost at least sixty-three by now," Kelpie said.

"Pixie post!" called a bright voice close behind them.

A small pixie wearing a smart brown hat and green leaf coat was standing at the door with two bulging grass-weave bags over his shoulder. He was having difficulty keeping his hat on as the wind gusted around the flowerpot.

Ping sat up straight. *It was going to arrive today*. She knew it. She felt the thrill of her secret fluttering inside her like a pair of tiny wings.

"Oooh!" said Brilliance. "I wonder if there's anything for me?"

"Who'd want to write to you?" Kelpie asked.

The fairies watched in excitement as the pixie walked up and down the Dining Flowerpot, distributing leaf letters and petal cards from his grass-weave bags. There was a fashion catalogue for Lord Gallivant and several (early) flutterday cards and parcels for Dame Fuddle. There was a tub of ant food for Bindweed the garden pixie, whose team of leaf-cutting ants clustered around his feet and sniffed at the tub in excitement. There were letters and magazines and pixie postcards. A number of letters fluttered out of reach, and swooped about in the wind as the fairies tried to catch them.

"Something here for you," said the post pixie, stopping at the Naughty Fairies' table.

"I knew I'd get something today," said Brilliance triumphantly. She put out her hand for the pale orange leaf that the post pixie was pulling out of his bag.

"Not you," said the post pixie. He handed the orange leaf to Ping. Then he tipped his hat at Ping and walked unsteadily out of the door. The wind blew up his leaf coat and lifted him off the floor.

"What is it, Ping?" asked Tiptoe with interest, staring at the orange leaf in Ping's hands.

"It's my magazine," said Ping casually. Her heart was pounding with excitement.

The fairies looked alert.

"What magazine?" asked Nettle.

"Since when do you order magazines by pixie post?" Brilliance demanded.

Ping shrugged. "Since Pong went into hibernation," she said. "It's so boring here without my dragonfly. So I thought I'd order a magazine."

"What kind of magazine is it?" Sesame asked.

"It's a very special kind of magazine," said Ping, folding up the leaf very carefully and putting it in her pocket.

The other fairies' eyes boggled.

"What's so special about it?" Brilliance asked.

"Give us a look," said Kelpie.

"No," said Ping. "Not yet."

Her friends groaned.

"Is it something you shouldn't have?" Sesame whispered.

Ping smirked. "Maybe," she said. "Who wants another clover bun? I'm starving."

2

Tooth Fairies
and Ladybirds

"Save me a place in Fairy English, will you?" Ping said, as they left the Dining Flowerpot.

And before the others could ask any more questions, she hurried across the courtyard. The wind tugged and pulled at her wings and her clothes. Ping kept her hand clamped across the leaf in her pocket and jumped into the air.

The wind almost flipped Ping upside down. She fought hard with her wings so that she blew quickly towards the sheltering Hedge, where she landed on a pile of dry brown leaves.

Then, and only then, did Ping take out her magazine.

Mischief Monthly was Ping's kind of magazine. Packed with magic tricks, jokes, pictures and stories, it gave Ping a million ideas for mischief. She read the magic tricks section as fast as she could. When she reached the bottom of the page, her eyes gleamed.

"Perfect!" Ping murmured to herself.

Ping sauntered into the English Flowerpot ten dandelion seeds later.

"Where have you been, Ping?" asked Dame Honey, the Fairy English teacher.

"It was the wind, Dame Honey," said Ping, sliding into a seat next to Brilliance. "I nearly ended up in the Pond. Sorry I'm late."

"We've only just started," said Dame Honey cheerfully, "so you haven't missed anything. Brilliance will explain what we're doing today."

"You fibber," said Brilliance as soon as the Fairy English teacher turned away. "You've been reading that magazine."

Ping sighed. She didn't want to tell Brilliance about *Mischief Monthly*. She wanted it to stay a secret.

"I won't tell you what we're doing if you don't tell me about your magazine," Brilliance hissed.

"Fine," said Ping. "Tiptoe will tell me. Won't you, Tiptoe?"

"It's a re-enactment," said Tiptoe. She ignored Brilliance's furious glare.

14

"About a tooth fairy. I think Dame Honey wants to prepare us for Dame Cavity's visit." She passed Brilliance a sheet of petal paper. The paper had a list of characters on it.

"What's everyone going to be?" Ping asked, reading the characters.

"Brilliance is the tooth fairy," said Nettle. "I'm the Child that's lost a tooth. You've really got to use your imagination on that one, Dame Honey said. Children are the biggest things you've ever seen."

"OK," said Ping. "What else?"

"Everyone else is an obstacle in the tooth fairy's path," said Nettle. "Except for Sesame. She's a ladybird."

Sesame beamed.

"What's so special about ladybirds?" Ping asked.

"Nothing," said Kelpie. "Sesame just wanted to be one."

Ping frowned at the list of characters.

There didn't seem to be much left. "So what about me?" she asked.

Brilliance smirked. "You're the tooth," she said. "I'm sure you'll be brilliant as that, Ping."

Soon, all the bark tables and acorn chairs had been pushed to one side to make room for the re-enactment. Brilliance stood at one end of the flowerpot, while Nettle lay on Dame Honey's desk at the other end. The rest of the fairies stood between Brilliance and Nettle, pretending to be wind, rain, thick grass, hungry hedgehogs, birds and firmly closed windows. Sesame was crouched in an unconvincing ladybird-shaped ball on the ground. Flea buzzed overhead, adding his own flavour to the re-enactment.

Ping lay underneath the table, pretending to be the tooth. It wasn't hard. All she had to do was lie there.

She closed her eyes and thought about the fantastic trick she was going to play that afternoon.

Dame Honey clapped her hands. "Off you go!"

"The Child has lost her tooth!" Brilliance shouted. "And I, Tooth Fairy of Tooth Fairies, am going to get it!"

Opening her eyes, Ping watched Brilliance march down the flowerpot. She pushed aside the grass fairies,

dodged the hedgehog fairies and blew
back at the wind fairies. The bird fairies
pulled back nervously when Brilliance
glared at them.

"Nothing stops the Tooth Fairy!" she
said in her most heroic voice.

"Except ladybirds," said Nettle in a
low voice to Ping as Brilliance tripped
over Sesame.

"Tooth fairies meet many obstacles on
their tooth-fetching missions," Dame

Honey said, helping a cross-looking Brilliance to her feet. "The wind can blow them off course. The rain can soak their wings and make it impossible to fly."

Tiptoe, who was pretending to be a raindrop, swelled up with pride.

"And the windows can be the worst of all," Dame Honey added, as Brilliance pushed Tiptoe out of the way and marched up to the final obstacle.

"Move, Kelpie," said Brilliance.

"No," said Kelpie, folding her arms. "I'm a window."

Brilliance tried to push Kelpie out of the way, but Kelpie wouldn't budge. Brilliance threw herself at Kelpie. The two fairies tumbled to the ground.

Dame Honey separated them. "Brute force won't work, Brilliance," she said. "You must use your imagination."

"I imagine a hole in the window," said Brilliance. She glared at Kelpie.

"Even if all the windows and doors of a House are closed, tooth fairies can always find a way inside," said Dame Honey. "Chimneys, ventilation fans, keyholes. We have the advantage of our size. You can move aside now, Kelpie."

Reluctantly, Kelpie stood aside.

"Aha!" Brilliance boomed. "The Child sleeps!"

"Not if you talk that loudly, she doesn't," said Nettle, opening one eye.

Brilliance pulled out her wand. She glanced at Dame Honey for more instructions.

"That's right, Brilliance," said Dame Honey. "Use your wand to take a puff of the Child's breath. You use this breath to lift the Child's pillow and reach the tooth that's underneath. The magic word is on the rockboard. Of course, it doesn't work on fairies, just Children."

"*Gypsofila!*" Brilliance shouted.

Underneath the table, Ping felt the magic shiver through the air.

"Now puff the Child's breath under the pillow," Dame Honey instructed, "and reach in for the tooth."

Brilliance waved her wand in a puffing sort of way.

"Say the magic word backwards,"

Dame Honey reminded her.

"Um," said Brilliance, squinting at the rockboard. *"Alifospyg?"*

The magic shivered again. Nettle obediently turned over. Brilliance reached under the table and pulled Ping to her feet.

"Leave the silver and put her in your toothpack," said Dame Honey.

Brilliance laid the silver fairy coin on the floor and Ping hopped on

Brilliance's back. Brilliance carried her unsteadily back down the flowerpot. The other fairies cheered.

"Well done, everyone," said Dame Honey, when the bark tables and acorn chairs had been pulled back to their usual positions and all the fairies were sitting down again. "Any questions?"

Kelpie glanced at Brilliance. "Are ladybirds usually such a problem for tooth fairies, Dame Honey?" she asked.

3

Not Bikini Weather

"I wish you'd tell us about your magazine, Ping," said Sesame, as they sat down for lunch. "Why does it have to be such a secret?"

"Naughty Fairies tell each other everything," Brilliance added, staring crossly at Ping.

"This one doesn't," said Ping. "Look, I'm planning something really big. That's all I'm going to tell you."

"Ooh!" Sesame squeaked with excitement.

Ping felt in her pocket, to make sure she still had the tiny ball of acorn powder, touch-me-not and beardgrass that she'd made that morning. "Watch

26

this," she murmured, and got to her feet.

The Naughty Fairies watched as Ping marched towards the staff table.

"What can we do for you, Ping dear?" said Dame Fuddle.

"I just wondered," said Ping earnestly, "if you could mention something to the other fairies at SPARCLE this afternoon." Discreetly, she dropped the acorn, touch-me-not and beardgrass ball into Dame Fuddle's elderberry juice. It fizzed briefly.

"Of course, my dear!" Dame Fuddle said, unaware of Ping's actions.

"Provided that it is a sensible something," murmured Dame Lacewing, Deputy Head of St Juniper's and the scariest teacher in the school. "I'm not hopeful."

Ping turned wide eyes to Dame Lacewing. "I wanted to raise awareness of the near extinction of the black bean

bug," she said. "It's a cause that's close to my heart."

Dame Fuddle looked moved. Dame Lacewing looked disbelieving.

"Of course I will mention it!" Dame Fuddle said, patting Ping's hand. "There will be many influential fairies present, after all! It's not . . . quite the usual sort of topic we discuss at SPARCLE, but it won't do any harm to shake things up a bit!"

Ping sauntered back down the Dining Flowerpot and rejoined her friends. Dame Lacewing watched her with a thoughtful expression on her face.

"You put something in Dame Fuddle's drink!" said Sesame, wide-eyed with admiration. "I saw you!"

"Maybe," said Ping.

At the end of lunch, Dame Lacewing rose to her feet. "As you all know," she announced, "Dame Fuddle is representing St Juniper's at the prestigious SPARCLE this afternoon. The school will assemble in the courtyard after lunch, to give Dame Fuddle a good school send-off. She takes the reputation of St Juniper's with her."

Dame Fuddle blushed and smiled as the fairies clapped.

"Your oh-such-a-big-something spell isn't working, Ping," said Brilliance smugly as they cleared away their plates.

"Isn't it?" said Ping.

They all filed out of the Dining Flowerpot. A bald dandelion clock stood sadly in the middle of the courtyard, its seeds scattering madly in the wind.

Dame Fuddle looked agitated as she stared at the dandelion clock. "Must go!" she twittered. "Mustn't be late!"

The fairies cheered as Dame Fuddle rose unsteadily in the wind. Dame

Fuddle waved, turned in mid-air and headed towards the Hedge and the Meadow beyond, where SPARCLE was taking place.

"Inside!" Dame Lacewing commanded. "Out of this wind before someone blows away."

Giggling and pushing, the fairies went inside.

"Time for the best bit," Ping said casually, pulling Brilliance back.

The Naughty Fairies looked alert. Dame Fuddle could still be seen, fighting against the wind as she flew towards the Hedge.

As soon as the last fairy had gone inside, Ping put out her fist.

"Naughty Fairies," she said.

This was the fairies' code for mischief.

"Ninja fruitbat," said Kelpie, putting her fist on Ping's.

"Nippy flipflops," said Brilliance.

"Needless fritter!" This was Tiptoe's.

"Gnawing figs."

"Gnawing starts with a G, Sesame," said Nettle patiently. "Nimble frogs."

"Fly, fly, to the SKY!" the fairies chanted together, and lifted their fists into the air.

"Watch this," said Ping. She pointed her wand at Dame Fuddle. "*Quercus polypogon!*"

Sesame screamed. The others stared.

"Dame Fuddle's wearing a bikini!" said Nettle in shock.

"An *acorn-cup* bikini," Ping said.

"She must be frozen," said Tiptoe in awe.

"It's not real," Ping said cheerfully. "It's a glamour. It looks like something it isn't. Dame Fuddle's still wearing real clothes. It just *looks* like she's wearing a bikini."

"But – what about SPARCLE?" gasped Sesame.

Ping smirked. "What about it?"

"They'll see Dame Fuddle . . . like *that*?"

"Yup," said Ping.

"Well, well, well," said Kelpie. "It's official, Ping. You are the naughtiest fairy I've ever met. And I've met a few. Myself included."

Ping swelled with pride. Kelpie, Tiptoe and Sesame were looking at her as if she was someone they'd never even met before.

Dame Fuddle had reached the Hedge. Her bikini strings looked like they were fluttering in the wind.

"I don't like this," said Nettle.

"Where's your sense of humour, Nettle?" said Ping, linking arms with Sesame. "They do glamours all the time in China."

Brilliance looked sour. "You've never been to China."

"So?" Ping said airily. "It'll be fine. No one knows it's me. I'll get rid of the

magazine, and that'll be that. Come on.
Let's go back inside."

"It was *here*," Ping said moments later
as she stared at her bedside table in
dismay. "I put my magazine here."

"Well, it's not here now," said Kelpie.

The fairies stared around the room.

"Maybe Dame Lacewing's found it,"
said Tiptoe nervously.

"Not good," said Nettle, shaking her
head.

"Not good at all," Brilliance added,
looking smug. "You're in for it now,
Ping."

"Well," said Ping, after a moment.
"We'll just have to act innocent if
anyone asks us about it."

"Us?" said Nettle. "What's this us?"

"You said the Naughty Fairies code,"
Ping reminded her. "We're in this
together."

"Something *you* forgot when you

36

didn't let us in on the fun and tell us about your magazine," said Brilliance moodily.

"Shut up about the stupid magazine, will you Brilliance?" Ping snapped. "It was *mine*. I could keep it a secret if I wanted."

There was an uneasy silence.

"Maybe the glamour will have worn off by the time Dame Fuddle reaches SPARCLE," said Sesame.

"Hope not," said Kelpie. "Imagine all those Senior Peris' faces when Dame Fuddle turns up in a bikini." The bluebells in the courtyard started ringing.

"Lessons already?" said Brilliance in disgust.

"It's the wind," said Tiptoe. "It's blown off the dandelion seeds quicker than normal."

"We'd better run if we want a seat at the back of Fairy Maths," said Sesame.

"I don't want to look Dame Lacewing in the eye today."

"I'll look her in the eye," Ping boasted. "I'm not scared."

"We know," said Nettle gloomily. "We can tell."

4

Trouble

"Ping," Dame Lacewing barked. "I will ask the question again. Are you listening this time?"

"Sorry, Dame Lacewing," said Ping politely. "I was miles away."

"That can be arranged," said Dame Lacewing in a dangerous voice. "So. If five post pixies are carrying five postbags, and each bag contains thirty-three leaf letters, how many letters are there?"

"Are the post pixies carrying five postbags each?" Ping asked.

"They are two-armed pixies," Dame Lacewing told her sternly, "not eight-armed octopuses. They have one postbag each."

"One hundred and two," said Ping.

Dame Lacewing looked perplexed.
"And how did you reach one hundred
and two?"

"I added up the letters," said Ping.

"You added them up wrong," said
Dame Lacewing. "The pixies are
carrying one hundred and sixty-five
letters."

"Oh!" said Ping. "I thought you
meant the letters in your question,
Dame Lacewing. There are one
hundred and two of *them*."

There was silence as everyone
counted the letters in Dame Lacewing's
question. Ping was right.

"So if you thought *that* was my
question," Dame Lacewing said at last,
"then why did you ask how many bags
each pixie was carrying?"

"I was just making conversation,"
said Ping.

Dame Lacewing put her head in her
hands.

"Look!" said a fairy near the front of
the classroom. "Dame Fuddle's coming
back."

Dame Lacewing looked up. "Already?
But SPARCLE has only just started!"

Other fairies went to the window.

"Why has Dame Fuddle got a leaf wrapped round her?" someone asked.

Because she doesn't want anyone else to see her acorn-cup bikini, thought Ping. She felt a thrill of terror run through her.

Brilliance rolled her eyes. "Here we go," she said.

"Hey, this is the fun part," said Kelpie, snuggling her feet deeper into Flea's warm fur under the desk.

"It's only fun if you know you won't get caught," Nettle pointed out.

Dame Lacewing rose from her seat. "Page twenty of your books," she said. "The chapter entitled Pixie Maths. I want at least ten sums from each of you by the time I get back."

As soon as Dame Lacewing had left, the fairies started talking.

"We're in so much trouble," Brilliance predicted. She glared at Ping.

"Oh, you know Dame Fuddle," said Ping. "She never gets cross about anything."

"No one's ever sent her to SPARCLE in an acorn-cup bikini before," Nettle reminded her.

"You're such a spoilsport, Nettle," said Ping crossly. "Why can't you enjoy the practical joke like everyone else?"

The other Naughty Fairies looked white-lipped and nervous. Even Kelpie.

"I don't see anyone enjoying themselves," said Nettle. "Do you?"

As there was nothing else to do, the fairies turned to page twenty and started adding up pixies. Ping was on her sixth sum when Dame Lacewing marched back into the classroom. The expression on her face was terrifying.

"Dame Fuddle has summoned the entire school to the Assembly Flowerpot. You will leave your books and follow me. In SILENCE."

The Assembly Flowerpot was only used
on special occasions. It was tall and
stately, and had fewer cracks than most
of the flowerpots at St Juniper's. All the
fairies in the school sat cross-legged on
the floor and stared up at the brick
which acted as a stage.

Dame Fuddle was standing in the
middle of the brick. There was no sign

of the bikini any more. Dame Lacewing stood on Dame Fuddle's left, and a large, comfortable-looking fairy in a rustly red leaf gown stood on her right. The other members of staff patrolled the Assembly Flowerpot, tapping their hands with their wands and glaring at any fairies who were whispering.

Dame Fuddle's usual vague smile had been replaced by a dark frown and a trembling chin. "Fairies of St Juniper's," she said, when everyone was seated. "I stand here today, deeply ashamed of this school."

"She's not talking in exclamation marks," Brilliance muttered.

"I *told* you it would be bad," Nettle hissed at Ping.

"Today," Dame Fuddle continued, her voice rising, "I was made to look a fool in front of some of the most important fairies in the land. And why? Because a St Juniper's fairy thought it would be funny to cast a spell on me."

The large fairy in the rustly leaf gown leaned over and patted Dame Fuddle on the arm.

"My sister Dame Cavity," said Dame Fuddle, her voice breaking slightly as she returned the large fairy's pat, "has been of great comfort since she arrived this afternoon and broke the spell."

"A monstrous trick," said Dame Cavity, in a rustly voice that matched her dress. "Not the kind of behaviour I expect to see at St Juniper's."

"You can tell she doesn't come to St Juniper's very often," Kelpie whispered to Ping.

"So now we are left with the sad duty of finding the fairy who was responsible for this outrage," Dame Fuddle continued.

"Dame Lacewing's looking at you, Ping," said Sesame in a low voice.

"She's still trying to work out if I did

that letter sum wrong on purpose," said Ping. "Don't worry. She doesn't know it's me."

Dame Fuddle's neck was beginning to wobble. "Lessons will continue as normal, except that we shall call every single fairy for an interview here in the Assembly Flowerpot. We shall find the culprit. And make no mistake!" The exclamation marks were back. "We shall find them and expel them! We shall show no mercy!"

And she burst into tears. Dame Cavity put her arm around Dame Fuddle and led her off the stage. The Assembly Flowerpot erupted with chatter.

"Poor Dame Fuddle," Tiptoe murmured.

"I've never seen her so upset," said Sesame, looking pretty upset herself.

"I guess it must have been pretty embarrassing," Kelpie murmured.

"I *told* you I didn't like this," Nettle

burst out. "I *told* you it was a joke too far."

Ping suddenly felt anxious. "You won't tell on me, will you?" she asked, staring at her friends.

"Of course not," said Brilliance after a pause. "Naughty Fairies stick together."

The other fairies nodded. But none of them looked Ping in the eye.

It was an anxious afternoon for Ping as, one by one, the fairies of St Juniper's were summoned to the Assembly Flowerpot. Lessons were strained, and the atmosphere gloomy and suspicious.

As they all sat down to a silent supper in the Dining Flowerpot, Sesame was called for questioning. Ping's appetite had disappeared. She pushed her cold roasted daisy heart round and round, leaving a smear of rosemary gravy on her plate, and waited for Sesame to come back.

"Well, that was easy," said Sesame, plonking herself next to Ping. "I just

told the truth. Mind you, Dame Fuddle wasn't concentrating on my answers much. She kept checking the dandelion clock out in the courtyard, like she was waiting for someone."

"Kelpie!" Turnip the kitchen pixie barked from the Dining Flowerpot doorway. "They want ye next."

Ping pushed her daisy heart around again. She kept thinking about her missing magazine. Where was it? Because it had come by pixie post, it had her name on it. If the teachers found it . . . She forced herself to eat a daisy heart. If they expelled her, she'd have to go home – and if she went home, she'd leave all her friends – and Pong loved it here and would bite her if they left . . . Ping's thoughts ran on a gloomy wheel, round and round.

"Tiptoe!" Turnip called, as Kelpie came back into the Dining Flowerpot.

"What did they ask you, Kelpie?" Ping

asked urgently, as Tiptoe left the room.

"Oh, stuff about spells and glamours," said Kelpie.

"Who was asking the questions?" Ping said. "Was Dame Cavity there?"

"She went off on her tooth mission ages ago," Kelpie said. "It was all the teachers, sitting in this long, scary row. Your basic nightmare. I kept smiling at Dame Honey and hoping for the best. Anyway, it was obvious I didn't know anything about glamours."

"If you knew about glamours, you'd have glamoured yourself ages ago," Brilliance said. "No one would wear such an ugly dress on purpose."

"I made this dress from Flea's fur," Kelpie said hotly, looking down at her black and yellow dress. "If it's good enough for Flea, it's good enough for me!"

They finished supper and walked through the buffeting wind to their dormitory. The wild, dark night suited Ping's mood, and she lay silently on her bed as the others talked. When Tiptoe came back, it was Nettle's turn – and then Brilliance.

"Bet you wish you'd told me about your magazine now, Ping," said Brilliance sweetly. She marched out of the dormitory.

Ping's stomach lurched.

"It's just Brilliance's way of getting back at you for keeping secrets from her," Nettle said. "She won't say anything."

"Easy for you to be so sure," Ping muttered.

Brilliance came back, accompanied by Dame Lacewing. Ping tried to catch her eye, but failed.

"Ping," said Dame Lacewing, consulting her list. "Come with me."

"Good luck," murmured Nettle.

"Who needs luck?" said Ping, as

jauntily as she could. Then, with quaking wings, she followed Dame Lacewing out of the dormitory.

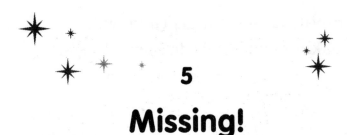

5

Missing!

"This should be an interesting conversation, Ping," said Dame Lacewing.

Ping followed Dame Lacewing across the dark, blustery courtyard. She kept her wings tightly furled to her sides.

"For instance," Dame Lacewing said, "you were the last fairy to speak to Dame Fuddle before she flew off to SPARCLE. What did you talk about again? The yellow bean bug? Or was it green?"

For a ghastly moment, Ping couldn't remember. "It was black," she blurted. "The extremely rare black bean bug."

"Of course," said Dame Lacewing

easily. "Silly of me to forget. I always thought they were rather common around here."

She pushed open the door of the Assembly Flowerpot.

Ping stared at the long table on the brick stage. It was lit by several fireflies, and it was completely empty.

"Dame Lacewing, thank goodness you're here." Lord Gallivant came rushing out of the shadows. "Dame Fuddle has had a funny turn. After the last young fairy left, she started crying, saying something about Dame Cavity."

Dame Lacewing rolled up her sleeves. "Stay here, Ping," she said curtly, before following Lord Gallivant to a dark corner of the flowerpot.

"Maybe I can help, Dame Lacewing," Ping offered, following closely.

"Unlikely," Dame Lacewing said. But she didn't send Ping away.

Ping's eyes grew accustomed to the

gloom. She could see Dame Fuddle
lying on a bed of leaves, moaning
quietly. Dame Honey was sponging her
forehead with warm dew, while Dame
Taffeta massaged her feet.

"Whatever is the matter, Fenella?" Dame Lacewing asked. "Bindweed, for Nature's sake, get some light over here."

Bindweed brought two fireflies over to Dame Fuddle's leaf bed.

"It's my sister!" Dame Fuddle sniffed. "She should have been back from the House several dandelions ago! I felt a dark shadow come over my heart just before you returned, Lavender! She's in terrible trouble, I know it!"

"How can you be so sure she's in trouble?" asked Dame Lacewing.

"She's my *sister*!" said Dame Fuddle piteously. "I *know*!"

Everyone had forgotten Ping. She backed away slowly and slipped out of the Assembly Flowerpot door. Then she ran as fast as she could, back to the dormitory.

"Back already?" Brilliance grunted. "I thought *you'd* be ages."

"Dame Cavity's in trouble," Ping panted. "We've got to get up to the House and find her."

"The *House*?" Sesame repeated in astonishment. "But . . . there are *People* in the House!"

"Duh," said Ping. "Come on, there's no time to lose!"

"What's Dame Cavity got to do with us?" Kelpie asked, looking up from grooming Flea's tummy.

"Don't you see?" Ping said. "Dame Lacewing *knows* I did the glamour. You should have heard the questions she was asking me on the way to the Assembly Flowerpot. If I rescue Dame Cavity, Dame Fuddle will be so grateful that she won't expel me!"

"You, you, you," said Brilliance. "It's always about you, isn't it Ping?"

Ping stared at her friends. "What?"

"The magazine was your secret," said Brilliance. "So was the glamour."

"Until you made us say the code," Nettle added.

"You wanted us to keep your secret when we were interviewed. Which we did, by the way. And now you want us to go up to the House," said Brilliance. "The most dangerous place a fairy can go. And all so *you're* OK."

"I didn't think of it like that," Ping said.

"We noticed," said Brilliance.

"I'm sorry I didn't tell you about my magazine," said Ping. "And the glamour. I thought . . ." She stopped.

"You thought you'd look better than us this way," said Kelpie. "Ping, naughtiest of Naughty Fairies. Right?"

"Yes," said Ping humbly. "I did. But I just look like someone who keeps secrets from her friends and then expects them to get her out of trouble. Don't I?"

No one said anything.

62

"Fair enough," said Ping, swallowing
a lump in her throat. "I got myself into
this, so I'll get myself out." She
marched over to the window and
unfurled her wings.

"You're not still going?" asked Tiptoe in surprise.

"On your own?" said Nettle.

"Up to the *House*?" shuddered Sesame.

"In the wind, and the rain?" said Brilliance disbelievingly.

"And past all those ladybirds," Kelpie added. Brilliance glared at her.

"Either I do this or I get expelled," Ping said. "Not much of a choice."

She put her foot on the windowsill. Then she felt a hand on her arm.

Brilliance winked at her and stuck out her fist. "Naughty fairies!"

The other fairies clustered round.

"Nougat fish."

"No friction!"

"Nasal fragrance!"

"Um . . ."

"Don't worry, Sesame," said Ping gratefully, putting her fist on top of Sesame's. "You'll only get it wrong.

Thanks, everyone. I don't deserve
friends like you. Nincompoops forever.
Fly, fly . . ."

". . . to the SKY!"

"And let's try not to get blown into
next-door's Garden on the way," said
Kelpie.

And the six fairies leaped out into the
darkness together.

The wind tossed Ping around like a

pancake. She forced her wings up and down, trying to remember everything that she knew about flying in bad weather. *Turn with the wind . . . Keep away from the raindrops . . . Fly undercover where you can . . .*

She lost sight of the others as she banked steeply and ducked underneath some tree branches. She really didn't want to get blown into the Pond.

The House was getting closer. Ping's

stomach gave a nervous wriggle. Dame
Honey's re-enactment hadn't prepared
her for anything *this* big. Each brick
was higher than she was, and she
couldn't begin to count how many
bricks there were from the ground to
the sky. Windows loomed, black and
smooth and endless.

Ping landed on a windowsill and
pressed herself close to the brickwork.
At least she was out of the wind.

"Whoo," said Kelpie, dropping down beside Ping. "I *so* nearly got splatted by a raindrop."

Tiptoe tumbled out of the sky. Kelpie and Ping managed to grab her by her fingertips.

"Thanks," Tiptoe panted, looking white-faced. "Nasty down-draught."

Brilliance and Nettle zoomed in, pulling Sesame along with them.

"This is great," said Kelpie. She jumped up and let the wind press her against the window. "Look, I'm Lord Gallivant, stuck on the fence!"

The fairies giggled. Once you got used to the weather, it was quite exciting.

"There's a fan set into the wall up there," said Ping, pointing. "We can get inside that way."

"But the blades are spinning!" Sesame wailed. "We'll be cut to pieces!"

"No need to risk it," said Kelpie.

"Look, up there."

The top window was open. It was just
a tiny crack, but it was all the fairies
needed. Flapping and scrambling, they
tumbled through the gap – and into the
warm, dry air of the House.

6

In the House

"Pooh," said Kelpie. "It honks in here."

The room smelled of stale air, socks, old cheese and dirty pants. Everything was dark.

"What's that noise?" Sesame whispered in a trembling voice.

Beyond the curtain, something was growling.

"We didn't practise dogs," said Kelpie. "Do you think they're as difficult as windows?"

Ping pushed at the curtain and peeped round. "I can't see a dog," she said. "But I think the Child in the bed is snoring."

"That's snoring?" asked Tiptoe in

amazement. "It's so loud! How come the Child hasn't woken itself up?"

"Don't ask me," said Ping. "I'm not a Human expert." She peered a little more closely at the figure in the bed. "That's a seriously big Child," she said after a minute.

"Dame Honey said they were big," Sesame assured her, peeping round the curtain as well.

"*That* big?" Ping asked.

All the fairies stared at the bed.

"I'm going closer," said Ping.

She jumped off the window sill and flew over to the pillow. The figure in the bed gave a grunt and turned over. Ping's heart nearly jumped out of her chest. She stared. Then she flew back to the window sill.

"Do Children have moustaches?" she asked the others.

"Don't think so," said Kelpie.

"Then we must be in the wrong

room," Ping said.

The fairies could see a glimmer of light beneath the door.

"Through there!" Brilliance whispered.

If they got on their hands and knees, there was just enough room for the fairies to crawl underneath the door. One by one, they edged through and out on to the landing. "Great," said Kelpie, brushing down her knees. "Now where?"

There were three more identical doors in the hallway. Somewhere, the fairies could hear the steady booming sound of a ticking clock.

"Let's be logical," said Nettle. "What do we know about Children?"

The fairies tried to remember.

"They don't have moustaches," Sesame offered.

"They like sweets?" Kelpie suggested.

"They can't fly, but wish they could,"

Brilliance said.

They all stared at an enormous picture stuck on one of the doors. It showed a Human with a screwed-up face. Its head was touching a round black-and-white ball, and its feet were off the ground.

"That one's flying," said Ping.

"That's not a Child," Nettle pointed out.

"Maybe they can fly when they're a bit older," said Kelpie doubtfully.

"We can't sit here all night," said Ping. "Let's try that door anyway."

To their relief, the door was ajar. This room was similar to the one they had just left, but smaller and not quite as smelly.

"Look!" Tiptoe hissed, as soon as they had flown in. "Dame Cavity!"

The Regional Tooth Fairy was lying in a crumpled heap on the floor just beside the bed.

"What's happened to her?" Sesame wailed, as Ping tried to shake Dame Cavity awake.

"I don't know," said Ping grimly, shaking again. "I think she's unconscious, though."

The fairies prodded Dame Cavity with their wands. No one could think of a waking up spell. Then Kelpie knelt down and slapped her.

"Ow," Dame Cavity moaned, and opened her eyes. She stared at the six fairies clustered around her.

"What happened, Dame Cavity?" Brilliance asked, kneeling down.

"Someone slapped me," Dame Cavity mumbled.

"*Before* that," Kelpie said.

Dame Cavity shook her head. She still looked a bit woozy. "I don't know," she whispered. "I . . ." Suddenly, she opened her eyes. "It was the *breath*!" she wailed, and passed out again.

The fairies looked up at the Child. All they could see was its arm, flung out of the bed and hanging down just above them like a long, pale, tree branch.

Kelpie shook Dame Cavity. "What about the breath?" she demanded.

"Leave me alone," Dame Cavity mumbled.

"You said something about the breath, Dame Cavity," said Ping urgently.

Dame Cavity shuddered. "Never . . ." she whispered. "Never have I . . . such a *smell* . . ." And she burst into tears.

"There, there," Sesame said, rubbing Dame Cavity's shoulder. "We're here to help."

Dame Cavity seemed to see them properly for the first time. "But you're so *young*! What . . . possible help can you be?"

Brilliance looked offended. "We'll go away then, shall we?" she said.

Dame Cavity shook her head quickly. "No, no . . ." she whispered. "Fetch . . . fetch the tooth. I'm too weak . . . too weak to move . . ."

"OK," said Ping. "Tell us what to do."

"The spell . . ."

"*Gypsofila*," Brilliance remembered. "Right?"

"Get the . . ." Dame Cavity swallowed.

"The Breath. But take care! I've been a Regional Tooth Fairy for more dandelions than the Meadow has ever seen, and this Child's breath is the worst I've ever known. If . . ." She swallowed again. "If you breathe it . . ." She closed her eyes as if the thought of the smell was too much all over again.

"Got it," said Ping.

She flew up to the Child's head and hovered as far away from its mouth as she could. Extending her arm, she turned her head away. *"Gypsofila!"* And then she clamped her lips tightly together.

With a sigh, the Child's breath whistled and flowed into Ping's wand. Ping felt her wand shaking. She screwed her eyes tightly closed and concentrated on not breathing.

Now what?

She opened her eyes and stared down at her friends. Her eyes bulged at them.

What do I say next? What next?

Brilliance flew up to join Ping, holding her nose tightly with both hands. Ping mouthed frantically at her. *What do I say next?* Her head was booming with the effort of not breathing.

Brilliance took her hands from her nose. "Oh," she said. "The next bit of the spell? Um . . ." And without

thinking, she took a breath.

Ping watched in horror as Brilliance tumbled out of the air and down to the carpet, where she landed with a soft thud. Ping couldn't hold her breath much longer. She could see Kelpie shaking Dame Cavity again. Dame Cavity was saying something . . . Ping wished she'd listened more closely to Dame Honey's tooth fairy re-enactment . . . Now she was starting to see stars . . .

"Alifospyg!" It was Tiptoe, fluttering around Ping, holding her up.

"Alifospyg!"

"Alifos . . . pyg . . ." Ping gasped. Her
wand bucked in her hand. She felt
Tiptoe pulling her down, away from the
Child and back to the safety of the
carpet.

"Thanks," Ping panted, taking great
lungfuls of air. She didn't care that it
smelt stale and disgusting. To Ping, it
was the sweetest thing she'd ever
tasted.

"How's Brilliance?" she asked, when
she'd got her breath back.

"Out cold," said Kelpie. "But she'll be OK."

Ping looked up at the Child again. It seemed a very long way away. "I have to go and get the tooth now," she said, trying to look brave. "Give me the fairy coin and your toothpack, Dame Cavity."

Dame Cavity took off her toothpack and gave it to Ping. Woven tightly from grass and stuffed with sheep's wool, it was beautifully made.

"The coin's . . . in there," whispered Dame Cavity. "Take care. The tooth . . . mustn't be chipped. Put it securely in the toothpack . . . and come away."

Ping shouldered the toothpack. "Get ready to catch me if I fall," she said. She took a deep breath, and flew back up to the Child.

The Child had rolled over in its sleep. The corner of its pillow was hovering slightly above the mattress, as if by magic. Which of course, it was.

Ping put the fairy coin under the
pillow – and stared.

There wasn't just one tooth.

There were four.

7

By the Skin of Her Teeth

"Four?" Dame Cavity repeated. "All at once?"

"Yup," said Ping. "I could only fit one in your toothpack, Dame Cavity. How are we going to carry home the other three?"

"Four at once," Dame Cavity repeated in wonder. "Of course, with breath like that . . . It's clear that there's something very wrong with that child's dental hygiene . . . but *four?* And only one coin . . ."

"With breath like that," said Ping, "he's lucky to get it. So, how are we going to carry the other teeth home?"

Dame Cavity lay back on the carpet. "Find some more toothpacks," she mumbled. "Use your imaginations, I'm going back to sleep now." And she turned over.

"Don't slap her again, Kelpie," said Ping. "Let her sleep. We can find something by ourselves, right?"

"What if the Child wakes up and sees her and Brilliance lying on the carpet?" Nettle asked.

"Let's push them under the bed," Sesame suggested.

Tugging and heaving, the fairies pushed Dame Cavity and Brilliance into the shadows.

"I'll look downstairs," Ping said. "I've always wanted to know what a Human house looks like. Who's coming with me?"

"Me," said Kelpie. "Must be your lucky day."

"We'll look round up here," said

Tiptoe. Sesame and Nettle nodded.

"Meet back here as soon as you can," said Ping. "Find anything soft that we can turn into a toothpack. Good luck!"

"I don't like the air in this House," Kelpie muttered, as Ping followed her underneath the kitchen door. "It's all still and warm and – *wrong*."

"I suppose Humans like it," said Ping, standing up. "Look, Kelpie, up there!"

The two fairies flew up to the kitchen table and tugged at an enormous white tissue that was poking out of a tissue box.

"No good," Kelpie panted. "We're not strong enough. Let's try next door."

"Whoa," Ping muttered. "We're being watched."

An enormous tabby cat was observing them from a basket by the kitchen table. It narrowed its eyes and flattened its

ears. A soft growling noise came from
its throat.

"Nice cat," Ping stuttered.

"Look!" Kelpie shouted, waving her
arms. "A mouse! Over there!"

The growling noise increased.

"Stop waving your arms, Kelpie!"

Ping begged. "It's going to . . . oh no . . ."

The cat leaped on to the table. Paws and claws flashed, huge and soft and sharp all at once as the two fairies flung themselves into the air.

"Let's get out of here," Ping hissed. "*Now!*"

They streaked across the room, tumbling and swerving as the cat followed.

"A keyhole," Kelpie panted. "There!"

They sped through the dark key-shaped hole – felt a whisk of a paw –

and were through to the other side.

"I think I'm allergic to cats," said Ping, smoothing down her trembling wings.

"I bet the others would have panicked," Kelpie boasted.

"We did panic," Ping said.

"Only a bit," said Kelpie. "Hey, look at that!"

The fairies stared in wonder across the darkened room. There was a perfect, fairy-sized house standing in front of them.

"Are there such things as house fairies?" Ping asked.

Kelpie flew over to the shiny blue door and knocked. The house stayed silent. "If there are," she said, pushing open the door, "then they're out. This is amazing, Ping! You've got to come in here!"

Ping followed Kelpie. She stared at the neat flight of fairy-sized steps rising

in front of her, and the little pictures
that hung on the walls. Ping fingered
the strange little objects that sat on
perfect, fairy-sized tables in the little
rooms, and wondered what they were
all for.

"Kelpie?" she called, looking round.
"Where are you?"

"Upstairs," Kelpie shouted. "I've found something, quick!"

Ping climbed the stairs, feeling the smooth bannister under her hand. This was probably how fairy princesses lived, she thought, with soft carpets and wallpaper and a whole stable full of dragonflies outside.

She walked into a room with two little beds. The beds had soft quilts on them, and there were curtains at the windows.

Ping gasped. Something was lying in the beds!

"Don't worry," said Kelpie, pulling back the quilts. "They're not real."

Two dolls stared glassily at them. They were wearing little flowery dresses and had tiny white socks on their feet. Ping stroked one of the dresses in wonder.

Kelpie tutted. "Not the *dresses*," she said. "The *socks*."

Ping looked at the socks. They were

soft, and toothpack-shaped, and absolutely perfect.

"Quick," said Kelpie, busily taking the socks off one of the dolls. "Tiptoe and Sesame will be wondering where we are. The other door out of here is open. I already checked."

Ping took off the second pair of socks. "Coming," she murmured to Kelpie, who was already heading down the little stairs.

"Thank Nature," Tiptoe muttered when Ping and Kelpie flew back into the Child's bedroom. "We were getting worried. Did you find anything?"

Kelpie produced the socks and waved them in triumph.

"Dame Cavity, can you fly?" Nettle asked the Regional Tooth Fairy, who was now sitting up on the carpet.

"Yes," Dame Cavity croaked. "But I couldn't carry a puff of air."

"Tiptoe, Sesame, Kelpie and I will carry the teeth," Nettle said, making a quick decision. "Ping, you help Brilliance. The window's open in here, so we can get out."

Brilliance's eyes fluttered. "Where am I?" she said groggily.

"Up you get," said Ping, as the other fairies flew quickly to the window. She draped Brilliance's arm round her shoulder. "Can you fly?"

Slowly, Ping and Brilliance rose off the floor and followed the others.

Outside, the rain had stopped. Although the wind was still very strong, Ping found a current of air that practically blew them all the way back to the flowerpot towers of St Juniper's.

They landed lightly in the dark, wet courtyard. The others had already gone. Ping guessed that they had already taken Dame Cavity to see Dame Fuddle.

"Brilliance?" she asked. "How are you feeling?"

"Weird," Brilliance mumbled, folding away her wings unsteadily. "Did you get the tooth?"

"*Teeth*," Ping corrected with a grin. "Yup."

Brilliance gave a tired smile. "Brilliant. So you won't get expelled after all."

"Maybe," said Ping.

To tell the truth, Ping was still feeling nervous about that. There was the problem of the missing magazine. If the teachers had it, then she could rescue a hundred tooth fairies and still be in very serious trouble. It was the only proof that she had anything to do with the acorn cup bikini.

Brilliance suddenly looked properly at Ping. "Nice dress," she said.

Ping stroked her flowery outfit. "I know," she said. "This stuff's all the

rage in China."

"You've never been to China," Brilliance challenged her.

Ping wasn't listening. Something was fluttering through the air towards her. It zigzagged and twirled a bit, then came down to rest by her feet. Ping picked it up. Suddenly, she didn't feel the cold, the damp or the wind any more.

It was her copy of *Mischief Monthly*. She wouldn't be caught after all! She would stay at St Juniper's, and Pong wouldn't bite her for making him leave, and everything was totally fantastic!

Kelpie came running out of the Assembly Flowerpot, with Sesame, Nettle and Tiptoe close behind. "Dame Lacewing's coming!" Kelpie hissed.

Ping thrust the magazine behind her back.

"Ah," said Dame Lacewing, striding across the courtyard. She stared at Ping's new dress. Ping tried her best to

101

look innocent. "I was wondering where you'd gone, Ping. But I learn from your friends that you've been busy."

"We rescued Dame Cavity," Ping said, "and we brought back four teeth for her."

"Yes," said Dame Lacewing thoughtfully. "Very good."

"So," said Ping, looking hopeful. "Do you still want to talk to me, Dame Lacewing? About – that other thing?"

"As there is no evidence to prove you had anything to do with that naughty glamour," said Dame Lacewing, "and since you have now rescued Dame Fuddle's sister, I think we should call it even. Don't you?" And with a half-smile, she turned and walked back to the Assembly Flowerpot.

The Naughty Fairies all breathed a sigh of relief. Then Ping remembered her magazine.

"Look what I just found," she said

happily, passing her *Mischief Monthly* to the others. "You have to check out the spell for making flutterday cakes fly across the room. I thought we could try it at Dame Fuddle's flutterday feast tomorrow . . ."